SEEK TO EARN

SEEKING IN ROMANCE BOOK 6

KEKE RENÉE

304 PUBLISHING COMPANY

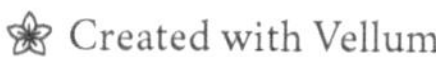 Created with Vellum

- Protecting Chanel (Special Forces Operation Alphas)
- Seek To Trust Book 5
- Seek To Earn Book 6

I WANT TO THANK first my readers for loving these characters so much and waited so love for them to come back.

ACKNOWLEDGMENTS

I CAN'T MENTION ENOUGH the support and dedication of my author buddies for keeping me uplifted. My behind-the-scenes team of beta readers, editors, designers, and more. As a writer, I continue to strive for the best, and I appreciate everyone who reads my work. Without your continual feedback, I wouldn't be on this path, letting doubts slip away.

INTRODUCTION

Are you signed up for my newsletter?

Join today and find out all the latest in new releases, contests, giveaways, sneak peeks, and more.

https://BookHip.com/BKRPJL

DISCLAIMER

THIS WORK OF FICTION contains strong language and explicit sexual content and is only intended for mature readers. This story may contain unconventional situations, language, and sexual encounters that may offend some readers. This book is for mature readers (18+).

SYNOPSIS

Falling for him would be a mistake, my heart can't take more pain.

Kadence:

I lost my husband, and my entire world turned upside down. All I could think about to keep from breaking down at night is my son.

Gunner comes into my life and shakes things up.

Can I keep my heart in check and avoid another heartbreak all over again?

Gunner:

Kadence is something I wasn't looking for, but I knew I needed her in my life.

We work together, but I don't think she really notices me. I can see the kindness in her eyes, but something is missing, and I want to make her smile again.

Will I be able to convince her that what she's missing is standing right in front of her?

CHAPTER ONE

GUNNER

Tonight, Club Seek was crowded, and the atmosphere was full of couples and singles ready to dive into unfiltered pleasure for the evening. I stood off to the side of the bar and lifted the bottle of Aces to pour two glasses for the waitress to take to the VIP room. Mason had been short-staffed, and I volunteered to handle the bar for a few hours. Normally, I'd give a refund to my clients, but Mason wasn't worried and knew how I did business. As the owner of Gunner Vishon Signature Bar and Staffing Services, I prided myself on having professional people work alongside me. To hear someone had taken advantage of my business relationship by constantly calling out or leaving early pissed me off. After Xavier introduced me to Mason, we became fast friends, and then he hired me to exclusively take on the bar upkeep and hiring for all of his clubs. Rosaline probably thought since we'd messed around in the past, she could get away with anything. I tried to be patient and understanding of her situation of not having family or friends in Tennessee, but I was done being nice to her ass.

A bottle girl approached and slipped a credit card on the bar with a receipt to pay the bill. I gave her back the card and saw another hand go up for a drink. I turned to pick up the bottle of scotch.

"Empty," I grumbled and tossed it back in the crate.

"Oops. Sorry." I heard a soft, angelic voice. I released one end of the crate and wrapped my hand around her elbow to prevent her from falling.

"Sorry, you okay?"

Her bottom lip curved into a sweet smile. She pulled her soft coils behind her ear.

"I'm fine. Sorry, I wasn't paying attention. My first day."

"What's your name?" I looked deeply in her eyes, wanting to know how to whisk her away from here.

"Gunner! Where's the vodka?" I swiftly turned my head at the stretched voice.

"Give me a second," I let Wendy know and released my hold on the newbie's arm.

"I should probably get back to my station." She shifted to walk around me, but I wanted to block her and get her name. The bar filled up, and Wendy pissed me off with her annoyed expression. I walked down the hallway, then pushed open the employee section and loaded up more scotch, vodka, and bottles of champagne. For a good moment, the girl I bumped into consumed my thoughts with her beautiful rich brown skin, the subtle lift of her full lips, and large brown eyes. I knew people said love at first sight and from that split second, I wanted to stare at her long lashes, curvy frame, and supple cleavage in the corset outfit all the bottle girls had to wear.

"You're still here." I gazed around to see Mason at the door.

"Rosaline called out again." I grimaced, lifted the crate up, and left the stock room.

"You need to fire her," Mason kidded, and I grunted and stepped back behind the bar to unpack the alcohol on the shelf. Mason reached down to grab a few bottles, placing them on top, and I poured the drink for Wendy so she could get going.

"Who's the new girl?" I asked.

"What new girl?"

I tapped him on the shoulder and pointed at the girl I ran into a few minutes ago.

"That's Kadence."

"What's her story?"

Mason grinned at me, and I clicked my tongue.

"Why?"

"I bumped into her by accident."

"She was hired two days ago, but I don't know much about her."

"Damn." She smiled in the face of a customer, and he reached a hand out and patted her on the ass. I wanted to say something, but she wasn't my girl. It would look suspicious if I punched him in the face.

"Listen, I need to get going before my wife calls and yells."

"We don't need Maya up here going off. How is she and the baby?"

"Great, it's nice to come home to a family."

"Family is what's important." My eyes went back to the new girl as she turned from taking an order, and we made eye contact. She smiled and then turned away when another customer grabbed her attention. Since everything seemed to be in order, Mason stepped from around the bar and headed to his office. I blew out a heavy breath and continued to help get the bar caught up. An hour later, I managed to get relief from another bartender and went to let security know I planned to leave for the evening. I pulled my phone out to check notifications as I walked out when Rosaline sent a message.

Rosaline: Sorry, babe. I'll make it up to you.

"Selfish," I mumbled and slammed in the back of someone.

"My phone!" she screamed and bent down to pick up her things.

"Shit, my fault." I reached down to help her, and she stood.

"You make it a habit of not paying attention when you're walking?" she asked, and I held her keys out.

"Only to beautiful women."

She shook her head and chuckled.

I held my hand out.

"Gunner."

She looked down at my hand and back up to me.

"Kadence."

We shook hands, and she whirled around to slide the key in a blue Kia Optima.

"Nice to meet you, Kadence."

"You too, Gunner."

I stared as she opened the car door and closed it behind her before putting on her seat belt. I debated if I should even try to question the flutter in my chest when this was only the second time we'd been in each other's presence. Most of my life had been about work and nothing else as I grew up wanting to be like my Dad and just focus on building a business. I had plenty of women in my life, but nothing was ever permanent or seemed to be fulfilling. Now to have this stranger completely cause peace and want inside of me had me second-guessing the future plans I laid out for myself.

"Have a nice evening, Kadence."

She backed out of the employee parking lot and drove

off as I watched until the taillights of her car faded away. Tomorrow, I had plans to hit the gym and maybe find out more about Kadence and her reasons for working at Club Seek. I slid into my car and headed in the opposite direction to my place. At the light, I picked up my phone and blocked Rosaline's number.

CHAPTER TWO

KADENCE

"Mommy, can we get pizza for dinner?" I pressed my lips together because this little boy loved to spend money he didn't have when I already had plans to cook dinner.

"Kyrin, I told you we have food at home, baby."

He groaned, and I tittered at the little attitude. He was like a grown man in a little boy's body sometimes. Other times, he was protective over me.

"Can we have it tomorrow then?"

"Boy!" I cackled and turned into the parking space of my mom's building. I'd spent all day with him before I had to work tonight at the club. Tonight would be my second night working there, and it wasn't for the bashful. I found out about the place through Emma because our kids went to the same daycare. She knew that with me rebuilding my life, I needed a job. My husband died suddenly a year ago, and I'd been struggling since to take care of my son. Kyrin, at four years old, reminded me of his father every time I looked at him. It took me a while to accept that his father was gone. Everything I planned for myself went into being

6

a wife and mother. When the path changed, life spiraled out of control. His parents never liked me, and it showed after his death when they basically disowned their grandson. They didn't give my son anything from the insurance money and refused to even tell me any of the plans. I managed to say my final goodbyes at the funeral before all hell broke loose when his mother tried to fight me.

"All right, we're here." I shut the car off and went around to grab him out of the car seat.

"I hope Granny has pizza."

I covered his mouth with my hand.

"Kyrin, you will eat whatever she cooked and maybe if you're good, I'll take you for pizza this weekend." I squatted down in front of him.

"And ice cream?"

The front door opened, and I stood.

"You finally showed up." Mom grumbled and leaned against the door with her arms crossed.

She wasn't a big fan of my new job and told me every chance she could. In her mind, I was stripping and needed something respectful.

"Hi, Mom."

"Hey."

Kyrin ran toward her and hugged her legs.

"Kyrin, be good for your grandmother." I grabbed his bag from the back seat and handed it to her.

"Okay, Mommy." He ran inside.

"When are you coming back to get him?"

"Tomorrow, if you don't mind." I felt a knot form in my stomach. Usually she'd complain once I picked him up.

"Kadence, you need a nine-to-five job like everyone else."

"Can we not do this today please?" I blew out a frustrated breath and got back in the car.

"Kyrin needs a stable environment." My lips parted and then closed.

"What do you mean a stable environment?"

"All this moving from my place and from job to job. Maybe you should think about contacting Kelvin's parents for help."

"Do you remember how they acted after his death? They don't want anything to do with me."

"I don't know what to tell you, Kadence, but I can't keep doing this with you." She turned to march back to her door. Growing up, she'd had men in and out her life after she broke up with my dad. He eventually remarried and had another family. He barely stayed in touch with me because she didn't like the fact he wanted someone else. I couldn't blame him because my mom was too judgmental and aggravating.

"I need to get to work."

Ring!

"Hello." I backed up out of the space.

"Hey, Kadence."

"Hi, Emma."

"You do remember me." She scoffed, and I laughed, stopping at the red light.

"Sorry, friend, life has been kicking my ass."

"Where are you?"

"Leaving my mom's house after dropping Kyrin off. Going home to nap and eat before work tonight."

"You sound like an old woman."

"I feel like one."

"You should come to lunch with me."

The light changed, and I sped up.

"I wish I could, but I have to save every dime I can get."

Emma's husband came from money, and they'd recently gone through some stuff. She told me at one point she was ready to leave her husband. I told her to make sure she had a backup plan. I knew firsthand that raising a child on your own was difficult if you didn't have a foundation in place.

"Lunch is on me, so stop stressing."

I checked the time on my watch.

"Okay, when is this lunch?"

"In thirty minutes."

"I'm not even dressed, Emma." I pouted and honked at the car that suddenly slowed down in front of me.

"Anything you wear shines. Stop pouting." Emma giggled.

"Fine, send me the address." We ended the call and a few minutes later, the address came through. I looked down at my shorts, crop top, and boots. My hair wasn't too off-putting, but I grabbed a little gloss and mascara to do a little touch-up.

Twenty minutes later, I arrived at a cute little bistro and parked my car. Emma told me she'd be near the back with some of her girlfriends. I shut and locked my door, strolled inside, and the hostess greeted me.

"Hi, How many in your party?"

"Actually meeting someone." I pointed to the three women sitting near the rear of the restaurant.

"Perfect! The waitress will be right over," the hostess said, and I nodded in answer.

"Hey, thanks for coming." Emma rose out of her seat and extended her arms for a hug. She shifted to the other women and introduced them.

"Nice to meet you, Kadence. I'm Chelsey."

"You too, Chelsey."

"Emma said you were cute, but, honey, you're gorgeous." Her other friend was named Maya and was a senator.

"Have to say the same about you, Senator." I smiled.

"Please call me Maya," she replied.

I scooted up to the table and placed my purse on my lap.

"What is my boyfriend doing?" Emma questioned, and I rolled my eyes. Emma spoiled Kyrin and whenever he went over to her place and spent the night with her son, he'd come back with more toys.

"Driving me up a wall."

Emma giggled.

"Her son is in the same daycare with my baby," Emma explained.

"You spoil him too much."

Emma waved me off.

"Don't hate on his swag," Emma joked, causing the entire table to burst into laughter.

"Where do you work, Kadence?" Chelsey asked.

"Club Seek." I dropped my head, embarrassed that I admitted it in front of a senator.

"Pick your head up. That's where I met my husband," Maya said, and my eyes widened at her comment.

"Mason owns Club Seek," Emma informed me, and I thought of Mason when I interviewed with him a few days ago. The man was cute, but the one I bumped into twice that day was insanely sexy. He was taller than me by a few inches, with short, wavy, golden hair, full bushy brows, and piercing gray eyes.

"I started a few days ago, and Mason's been really great."

The waitress came over and set their drinks down on the table.

"Are you hungry?" Emma asked.

"A salad would be fine and whatever they're drinking."

"A peach bellini," Emma said.

Chelsey and Emma started to drink, and mine showed up a second later.

"I know Maya is a senator. What do you do, Chelsey?"

"I work at my family's bank."

"That has to be exciting. Does your husband work there too?"

Chelsey's small, toothless grin formed on her face.

"He is a fitness trainer and owns his own gyms."

"Nice! But do you have to deal with women throwing themselves at him?"

Chesley snorted.

"All the time." She chuckled, and we laughed. For the rest of the afternoon, we exchanged numbers and went shopping, but I didn't purchase anything. My goal was to build up my money to get a new house one day. After my late husband's parents kicked us out of our old house, I lived with my mom until I could save up for an apartment. Once I fully had enough for a down payment, I wanted to get back in a home and focus on going back to school to get a degree in business.

CHAPTER THREE

KADENCE

I'd been working for a month now at the club, and I was late today because Kyrin started crying when I tried to leave him with my mom. I felt guilty, so I stayed until he fell asleep. I'd made enough to pay for school registration for a few classes, so we were in a routine now. In the mornings, we had breakfast, and I dropped him off by nine at daycare. Three days out of the week, I went to class and then came home to clean and sleep. Then it was time to pick him up and drop off with my mom. I put my purse in the locker, checked my makeup in the mirror, and went to grab my tray and notepad. The outfits we had to wear weren't my favorite, but they were necessary when working in a place that alludes to sex and mystery. I worked on the main floor, but a few girls said when they had to work upstairs or in private sections, they'd come across a lot of naked bodies and had been invited to join. I was curious about the overall practice when someone joined, but being dominated during sex didn't appeal to me that much.

"We meet again."

I shut the locker and whirled around to find Gunner, a business friend of Mason's.

"Hey. Gunner, right?"

"It is, how are you?"

Another girl walked between us and left us alone.

"I'm fine. Just running a little behind."

"I'll put in a good word for you, Mason owes me."

Those thick lips curved into a smile, and his long tongue made an appearance when he swiped across his upper lip.

"If I let you do that, then I'd owe you." I crossed my arms.

"Nah, just a friend doing a favor."

"Oh, we're friends now."

"I mean we bumped into each other twice."

"So that makes us friends?" My brows dropped in confusion.

"Yes. and soon best friends. Then we will go out."

"Huh." I laughed at his statement.

"You're beautiful, Kadence. I'd like to take you out."

"Uhm, what makes you think I'm single, Gunner?"

"I don't, and I really don't care." He walked closer to me, and the laughter left my face. I cleared my throat and shook my head.

"You're too cocky for me, Mr. Vishon, and you're my boss."

"Call me Gunner, and I'm a silent partner."

"Which means, based on the rules, I shouldn't even be talking to you."

His eyes narrowed in on me.

"Mason found his wife here at the club, plus Warren and a few other people. Employee and employer relationships happen."

"They do, but I'm not in the habit of being the type to fall for the boss."

"Good because I'm not your boss." My heart was beating out of my chest at the look he gave me.

"Gunner."

He waved me off.

"One date, that's all I ask."

"You don't even know me."

"I know you're a single mom, in school, and focused on raising your son."

I stuck my hand on my hip.

"How do you know all of that?"

"Go to dinner with me, and I'll tell you," he said, stretching out a beckoning hand.

"All right, one dinner."

He smiled and kissed the back of my palm and walked out. For the rest of the night, I worked, but my mind was on Gunner and our date. I was afraid it would open a can of worms with Mason.

* * *

THE NEXT MORNING, I finished class early and decided to go to the mall to do a little shopping with Emma and her other friend Kyra, who I found out was a famous actress. In each store, a crowd of people would take pictures of us, and photographers stood outside the building.

"Tell me I'm crazy for even agreeing to this date." I stood in front of the mirror with a gold shimmery dress.

"No, I told you Maya and Mason got together there, plus me and Jordan."

"Emma, that's different. I'm a bottle girl, and he's practically my boss."

"From what you've said, he seems like a good guy," Kyra noted.

I sighed and put the dress back, flipping through the rack. "He's—"

"Cute, sweet, and knows what he wants. You've been alone for almost two years. Time to get out and do something for yourself," Emma said.

"I feel like I'm betraying Kelvin."

"Kelvin wants you to be happy."

"What if he hates the date, and we end up back at work, and it's weird between us."

"You've created this entire situation in your mind, and the date hasn't even happened." Emma stood next to me.

I felt goose bumps rise on my skin.

"What's the real problem?" she asked.

"I will end up falling for another person, and they leave me."

"Life is about living. You can't think like that, Kadence. Just one dinner, promise me you'll go." She held up her pinky finger.

"Are we ten years old or something?"

Kyra laughed at me.

"Yep, and you're going on this date. Who's watching Kyrin?"

"Mom, and I need to hurry up and get home and get dressed."

"If she acts crazy and says no, then bring him to me."

"Thank you. I like the light cream floral dress." I pointed to the dress on the second rack.

"With your hair pinned up, that would be cute," Kyra said. I nodded in agreement.

We all walked to the register and paid for our clothes. Afterwards, I went to get my nails done. Even though I wasn't planning on sleeping with him, I needed to be refreshed and glowing. It took me two hours to get dressed, do my hair, and finalize my makeup. Plus, I had to get Kyrin a bath at my mom's place and tuck him into bed. It was now nine-thirty, and I waited for Gunner to pick me up.

Ding!

The doorbell rang, and I jumped up and ran to the front door.

He whistled when he saw me, and I found myself blushing.

"You look beautiful."

"Thank you. You look handsome. I didn't know where we were going for dinner, so I hope this is okay." I motioned up and down at my dress. It wasn't too revealing, besides showing off my legs. I had on three-inch heels with my hair up, half of it hanging with flowing curls.

"The perfect dress for the perfect lady." He held a hand out and I extended for him to hold mine as I reached to close the door behind me.

"A limo!" I gasped in shock.

"I didn't want to lose focus tonight. All my attention will be on you, and driving would hinder that."

"But that's too much, Gunner."

"Let me worry about that." He opened the back door, and I climbed in. He followed and directed the driver to the restaurant.

"Why me?"

"Look, before we even get to the dinner, you should know I don't do things out of pity or to show off. I like you and want to get to know you. It's that simple."

"So, you're not looking to save me or lock me up as your sex buddy?" I watched him peer down at my lips, then back up to my face.

"Sex is easy to come across. I would like to know Kadence Wilkes and what makes her happy."

The limo arrived at the restaurant a few seconds later and parked.

"We'll call you when we're ready, Elliot." Gunner reached for the door handle, stepped out, and helped me next. We reached the front door and found it to be completely silent inside. I wondered if we came on a closed night.

"Uhm, are you sure the place is open?"

"I paid to have you all to myself and rented out the place."

"But—"

"Mr. Vishon, we have your table ready for you." The hostess escorted us to the middle of the dining room.

"You seem shocked by this, Kadence."

The table was decorated with candles, and a bottle of rosé sat in a bucket of ice.

"Speechless honestly."

"You shouldn't be. As we get to know each other more, you'll find that I don't half ass when I make someone my girl."

"What makes you think I'm going to be your girl?" I teased and cupped my chin with my hand on top of the table.

"I see you're intrigued by me, and I promise the night we ran into each other, I was intrigued by you."

He reached for the bottle and poured a glass for me, then him.

"This is the first date I've been on since my husband died. Before that, we were married for six years."

"Do you mind if I ask how he died?"

"Cancer. It's one of those things you don't prepare for. Then his family never liked me in the beginning, so it only caused a bigger strain."

"They're the fools." He covered my palm.

"Thank you. I have my son, so he's been great to keep my mind distracted."

"Kids can be the best things to bring you joy."

"Do you have any?"

"No. I've never thought of myself as a father."

"Oh." I didn't lie when I told him I hadn't gone on a date. I didn't want to bring different men in and out of Kyrin's life. If Gunner was to stick around, and he didn't like kids, this would end before it even started.

"Hey, I like kids. Just never thought of being a father until I saw you."

"Kyrin is my baby. If I brought anyone around, it would need to be someone special."

"Then I'm your man."

I laughed.

The waitress brought over appetizers of salad and mussels.

"Cocky."

"Confident."

"Tell me about you." I said.

"I invested a lot in business and became a small partner at Club Seek. Also, I run a staffing agency for clubs and events."

"Wow, that's exciting."

"I grew up with parents who worked and instilled that in me. When I went to school, I brought liquor and the girls."

"Frat boy." I smirked, and he fed me some of the mussels.

"Actually a nerd in school."

"You're lying."

"No, girls liked me, and I'm not playing innocent, but

nothing made a lasting impression."

"Until me."

"Until you."

"Doesn't it bother you that I was married and have a child? Not looking for a stepdaddy."

"I wouldn't expect you to, Kadence. I know I come on strong, but something is brewing, and I've seen you come to work. You seem to be on the go. Never take the time for yourself."

"Wouldn't even know what that feels like."

"How is working at the club for you? I mean it's an adult membership only."

"At first, I was hesitant. I'm not the most sexually outgoing person."

"So, I have to earn your pleasure."

"Well, we have to see how this first date goes."

"What do you do outside of work?" He changed the subject, as our food came out. We dove into the salmon avocado salsa and risotto.

"I went back to college to get my degree. I have two years left."

"That's amazing, smart and sexy." His words made me nervous and tingly all over. The words he spoke to me gave me confidence and strength to not let anyone's actions put me in a bad place.

The dinner was amazing. Then we walked around talking and ended up back at my apartment alone in front of my door. We stood face to face and held hands, and I felt like a teenager home from her first date.

"I had fun tonight." I spoke low.

"Me too, and I want to see you again."

"Maybe." I grinned, and he chortled, stepped closer to me, and rubbed right cheek.

"Can I kiss you, Kadence?"

Before he could even get the words out, I leaned forward and closed my eyes. We collided together, and his tongue opened my mouth. His moan caused me to pull him closer to my chest, and his hands went to my lower back. Our kiss went on for another few minutes before he pulled back.

"I'm sorry. I shouldn't have," I said, wiping the lipstick off his lips.

"I'm not. Get inside, and I'll call you tomorrow." He pecked my lips and waited for me to unlock the doors. I waved good night and leaned my back to the door and closed my eyes.

"Woah."

CHAPTER FOUR

GUNNER

"You went on a date?" Xavier asked, lowered the weights, and wiped his forehead. I got up extra early and came to the gym to release the tension from my date with Kadence. Her moans when I kissed her had me ready to fuck her right on the porch, but I didn't want to disrespect her home and son. So, I forced the kiss to end. Then I came home and jacked off in the shower and tossed and turned with her on mind.

"Yeah." I lifted myself up and did some sit ups.

"You and Rosaline only have sex. Since when do you take her out on dates?" Xavier chuckled.

"Never. It was with a bottle girl at Club Seek."

"Who?"

"Kadence, a friend of Emma and Chelsey."

"Awww. Gotcha." Xavier, like me, didn't care what the world said about who we should and shouldn't date because of different backgrounds. He came from a working-class family and married into a rich family. Her parents, at first, objected because he wasn't from wealth. I came from money and dealt with the pressures of people wanting me to fit into a box based on my family's status. But I liked to use my own mind, and my parents understood even though my grandparents came from money.

"Is she cute?"

"Hell yeah." I smiled at the thought of her.

"Are you ready to date after being single for so long? Especially someone you work with?"

"I want her."

He stopped lifting and turned to me.

"She a bottle girl or…" I stopped him before he even threw it out of his mouth. Some women did have experiences with men, and Mason had strict instructions on the type of people allowed.

"She's a bottle girl."

"Can't imagine dating a girl from the club."

"You fuck Chelsey at the club."

"That's different."

"How?"

"We're married, and she doesn't work there to see around-the-clock fucking."

"Kadence isn't like that. She's sweet, smart, sexy, and funny."

"Well, if she makes you happy."

"Besides, Rosaline doesn't mean anything to me."

"Does she know that?"

"I had a few texts from her come through the other night, and I told her it was over if she called out again."

"You fired her."

I nodded.

"What did Mason say?"

"He doesn't run my business."

"The man hired you to staff his bars at most of his clubs."

"Rosaline is good at her job, but she's not dependable."

"Good luck with that."

"Knew you two would be slacking off in here." Warren and Mason strolled in and laughed.

"That's him." Xavier pointed at me.

"He's still high on his date with Kadence." Mason laughed, and I flipped him off.

"Yeah, I heard the girls on three-way about you," Warren joked.

"Fuck y'all." I smirked.

"Does she know about the private rooms?" Xavier asked, and I shook my head. One of the reasons I kept Rosaline around was because she liked BDSM and what the club represented. We could explore each other and not have to worry about someone freaking out when they saw bar spreaders, whips, and cuffs. This world started for me in college, and I continued throughout and knew when I got married, I'd want someone compatible, who was open to the lifestyle just as much.

"I haven't talked to her about it yet."

"If you're really into her, you should start that conversation."

He was right, and I knew after one date, when we kissed, I wanted her for myself.

"Focus on someone else's love life," I blurted and stood to spot him on the weight bench.

"Kyra and I are trying for a baby," Warren said. We all hugged in excitement and congratulated him.

"Guess I'll be the sexy uncle to y'all kids," I joked, and they laughed.

* * *

A WEEK LATER, Kadence and I were on a fourth date, and it was a simple picnic at my house. I put on the fireplace and a movie with our food laid out in front of us. I wanted to have her alone to myself so we could continue to talk and learn more.

"Here's to you." Kadence held the glass of red wine up in the air.

"A toast for me." I watched her pull her bottom lip in and ran a hand through her long hair that she left down.

"I can admit you've been a pure gentleman through our dates, and you've grown on me."

"That's good to know. Anything else is love." I tapped her on the nose.

"Well, I have to admit I haven't had sex in a while besides a vibrator and my hand." She nervously shifted.

My eyes darkened at her confession.

"What's a while?"

"At least a year and a half since my husband died."

I was ready to take her right here but calmed my thoughts of bending her over the table.

"Have you ever been to the club as a guest?" I needed to see what her level of intimacy would be.

She choked on the wine, and I gently clapped her back.

"Are you okay?"

"Yes, so-rrrry… Uhm," she stuttered.

"Are you into the BDSM lifestyle, Kadence? Ever had a desire to join?"

"I mean, I'm not really sure. Mostly been into the regular smack on the ass and tug my hair."

We laughed at her comment.

"Would you ever like to go? With me of course." I put the glass down on top of the table.

"As a guest?"

"We'd take it slow and introduce you to my world."

"I don't want you to be disappointed."

"Unless this isn't what you want. But you could never disappoint me, baby."

"All right."

"All right." My dick got hard, and I pressed a kiss on her forehead, inhaled her hair, and trailed kisses along her cheek and shoulder. She caressed my chin and slid her tongue in my mouth. I trailed my fingers down her arm. She moaned when my hand went under her shirt. I inhaled her perfume and removed my hand.

"Tomorrow."

"I have work."

"I'll deal with Mason."

"But I need the money, Gunner." Her expression was annoying.

"Love, you'll make the same amount from me. Don't stress about that."

"I can't believe I'm actually doing this." I kissed her ear and down her chin to her lips.

"Already done, baby." Slowly, I kissed her while she talked about introducing me to her son.

She closed her eyes and interlocked our hands together. Then she pulled back, so I turned the movie up, and we continued to watch and hang out all night. She spent the night until the early morning, and I cooked breakfast, then drove her back home.

CHAPTER FIVE

KADENCE

Today, Kyrin decided to not drive me crazy, so I took him out for ice cream after we came from the library to pick out some books. He kicked his feet back and forth on the chair, and I saw specks of his father in his face and demeanor.

"Kyrin, how is daycare going?"

"Fun." His eyes rose with chocolate syrup on his chin. I cleaned his face with a napkin.

"I'm glad."

"Mommy, how is your school going?" Amusement glinted in his eyes.

I chuckled at his question.

"Mommy is doing good, baby."

"Then you should pick out some books for yourself."

I chuckled.

"Next time, baby."

"Grandma said you work too much at night."

I blew out breath. My mom and I didn't see eye to eye still with my job choice.

"Grandma shouldn't worry you, baby."

"Do you like your job?"

"Yes, and it pays for this ice cream. But you don't have to worry about that."

"Okay."

I watched him move the ice cream around.

"Hey, how would you like to meet a friend of mine?"

He shrugged.

"I know we haven't talked about your dad in a while."

"He's in heaven, right?" I cradled his face in my hands.

"He is and looks down on us every day." I wiped his hands clean.

"I miss him."

"He misses you too, baby."

"Can we go see Grandma and Poppa?"

I hated to be the bearer of bad news and have them shut the door in my face. I'd avoided this conversation for a year, but Kyrin remembered everything.

"Maybe in the future. Kind of hard for Grandma and Poppa to see us right now."

"Because Daddy is gone."

I nodded but wanted to say because they never liked me and thought I trapped their son.

"Finish your ice cream, and then we can go home and watch a movie."

"Okay, Mommy." Kyrin grinned, showing off his beautiful little teeth.

* * *

I GLANCED at the front door of my mom's apartment and saw the curtain move, so I knew she was here. I hadn't spoken to her in a few days. After I took Kyrin out for ice cream and the library, I asked Mason for a few days off to spend time with my son, and he agreed. After a month at the job, I was more comfortable with how things ran. I got along with the staff, and Gunner came in some nights when I worked even though he didn't need to be there.

"What are you doing here, Kadence?" Mom held her robe closed, moved to the side to let me in, and shut the door behind me.

"I wanted to see you."

"Where's Kyrin?"

"Daycare."

"No class today?"

"No."

"Surprised you aren't at work."

"How have you been?"

Her eyes scanned me up and down. Gunner bought me a nice bracelet and shoes. I wasn't the material type of girl, but he was spoiling me beyond my dreams.

"I met someone."

"I hope you're not pregnant, Kadence.

"What? No."

"Thank God. You've always been flaky and never listened to me growing up."

"How can you say that? If anything, I watched you and my father go back and forth arguing until all hours of the night."

She waved me off.

"Your father wasn't shit."

"Here we go."

"Listen to me, I did the best I could, and he just left."

"Mom, you have to let it go."

"Try to not run this one off."

"All I wanted to do is hang out with you and have lunch or something."

"You got some money."

"That's all you care about is money."

"I mean if you're coming in here with diamond bracelets and your hair all done, you must have a sugar daddy."

"Gunner is nothing like that." I reached in my purse, pulled out some money, and slapped it in her hands.

"When is Kyrin coming back over?"

I jumped off and stalked to the door.

"Tomorrow and try to keep my business out of your mouth." I slammed the door behind me and strolled to my car. I couldn't wait for my night with Gunner to let off some steam and deal with my mother. She tried to dictate my life and make me feel miserable, the same way her relationship with my father caused her misery.

CHAPTER SIX

GUNNER

I blocked out the red room for tonight, turned the low lights on, and talked to her about what we would be doing for the evening. She walked in wearing a long, black lace gown with a matching black bra and panty set. We watched a couple have sex first; then I pulled her to the private room and pointed to each item that I wanted to try with her tonight. The look in her eyes was interest, but she was nervous. Once her clothes came off, I placed a sinful ball in her mouth, then set the sex bench up for later. I held the spank paddle up and rubbed it over her smooth flesh and lightly tapped it against her right cheek.

"Ohh gosh, mmmhhmm." Her eyes closed, and I loved how she submitted to me easily and was open to testing her limits.

"Baby, remember your safe word if you feel over-whelmed."

I leaned over and swirled my tongue over her nipple, and slid an index finger inside her pussy, her wetness showed against my fingers.

"Kadence, love, you're so fucking beautiful," I whispered, warm breath against her chest.

Smack!

I moved my hand over the sting and kissed both cheeks. Spreading them apart, I dropped to my knees and slid my tongue in her pussy.

"Arghhh, Gunner." Her moans filled my heart, and my dick got hard. I spat in her ass and slowly slid my finger in and out. I sucked and twirled my tongue at the same time, moving my finger in again.

"Yes, baby." Her lips fell apart.

Her moans filled the air, her juices covered my beard, and she couldn't touch me while her hands were cuffed. Finally, I removed my pants, slid the condom on and eased into her tightness. I felt like I was home.

"Love, you're killing me."

I removed the ball gag and thrusted forward. She looked over her shoulder as I kissed up her back, then captured her lips.

"Arghhh… Shit!" I grunted and dug my hands in her waist and stroked her faster.

"Gunner, I'm coming," she screamed, and I felt her nectar cover my dick. I pounded until I came and my breathing was out of control. I slid out of her and removed her hands from the cuffs. She steadied her breathing, lying flat on the bench.

Thirty minutes later, I brushed a thumb over her soft, plump lips and glanced up to her eyes in need of a sign this was what she wanted. I got my answer when she rested a hand on my cheek, leaned forward, and crashed her lips to mine. I pulled her bottom lip in my mouth, sucking on it slowly, and she moaned, leaning her head back as she closed her eyes. I put on another condom, and she straddled my lap, and we made love almost all night.

* * *

TWO MONTHS PASSED, and we had a scheduled day for me to finally meet her son. I was at her door holding a train set and flowers. A part of me was nervous because most of the women I dated didn't have kids. Now, I was in a full-blown relationship, and I loved that her son was the top priority when we made any types of plans.

Knock! Knock!

"Here I come." I heard the door unlock, and Kadence stood in a pair of biker shorts and a long shirt, which brought back memories of our first night together.

"Hey, love."

"You didn't have to bring anything." She invited me in, and I kissed her and passed her the roses.

"For you."

"Thank you, Gunner. Is that train set for Kyrin?"

"Mommy! Who's at the door?" A little boy ran from the back and stood behind his mother's leg.

Kadence bent down.

"Baby, this is Mommy's friend. Can you say hi, Mr. Vishon"

"Hi, Mr. Vishon."

"Gunner. Nice to meet you, Kyrin."

"You know my name."

I bent down in front of them.

"I do. Your mom told me."

"Oh. What's that?" He pointed at the train set.

"I brought you a gift."

"Really!" He jumped up and down in excitement.

"I did. Hopefully, your mom says you can keep it."

She pursed her lips.

"I can't take it now, since it's here." Kadence and I stood.

"Yayy! I'm going to play."

"First you need to finish your food."

"But Mom…" he whined.

"No, Kyrin."

She pointed to the back, and I assumed the kitchen. Kyrin's face dropped in defeat, and he walked back to the kitchen with the train set.

"Hi." She leaned into my chest, and I wrapped an arm around her waist.

"Hey, baby." I kissed her on the lips.

"Mhmmmm. Come on, you hungry?" She pulled back before we got started and took my hand.

"Sure, I could eat." I stared at her ass.

"Food, Gunner."

Her eyes blazed with emotion, and I chuckled.

Kadence put the flowers in water, and I removed my jacket and sat down at the table across from Kyrin. He bit into the piece of fish, then mac and cheese.

"Kyrin, I hope you like the train set. I had one growing up just like that."

"Cool. I love trains and fire trucks."

"I'll remember that for next time."

"How do you know my mommy?"

Kadence put a plate down in front of me.

"We met at work."

"Kyrin, you remember I told you Mommy had a friend?"

He nodded.

"This is Mommy's special friend. I wanted him to meet you and get to know the number one guy in my life."

"That's me!" Kyrin stuck his hand in the air and laughed.

"Yes, you are, sweetheart," Kadence replied, and I winked. The way she talked and took care of him made me even more enthralled with her.

"Are you going to marry my mommy?" Kyrin asked, and we both froze.

"Where did that question come from, Kyrin?"

"Grandma said—" Kadence motioned for him to stop.

"Grandma shouldn't have brought that up to you. I'm not getting married. We're dating, baby."

"Okay."

"When or if that time ever comes, I would talk to you first, okay?" Kadence explained and I knew she was the entire package of what I needed in my life.

"The food is good, babe." I cut into the fish and took another bite.

"Thank you. After this, I have cupcakes for dessert."

"What are your plans for tomorrow?"

"Class and hanging out with the girls."

"How about we have dinner with everyone?"

"That could work. I only have two classes tomorrow."

"Great, then just come to my place afterwards."

"Can I come?" Kyrin asked and looked at his mom.

"No, baby. This is a grown-up dinner," she answered, and I wanted to say yes.

"We can take him to the park another day with just the three of us."

"Yeah, the park!" Kyrin clapped his hands.

"I can see you two stressing me out already," she said and helped him off the chair. He ran back to the living room with his train set.

"He's a good kid, Kadence."

"Thank you."

"You're doing a good job with him."

"I needed to hear that."

"You never have to worry."

Buzz!

When I felt my phone vibrate, I removed it from my pocket and saw a message from Rosaline.

Rosaline: Gunner, you really fired me!

Rosaline: Baby, call me back.

"Everything all right?"

I deleted her messages and placed my phone back in my pocket.

"Fine, babe."

"You sure?"

This was the third time Rosaline texted. I made it clear the last time not to be late.

"How is school?" I changed the topic, continued to eat, and listened to her goals.

"Good. My teachers are great and so far, I've passed my tests."

"You'll have a degree real soon, babe."

Kadence smiled and picked up her plate, along with Kyrin's, and took them to the sink.

"Are you ready for cupcakes and movies?"

"I'm ready for something sweet, but not cupcakes." I came up behind her and wrapped my arms around her waist.

She moaned when I nuzzled my face in her neck.

"Behave, Mr. Vishon."

"I can't promise you'll wear those shorts." I slapped her on the ass.

I helped her carry the cupcakes to the living room. We sat and watched *Spiderman* and a few Pixar animations for the rest of the night with Kyrin.

CHAPTER SEVEN

KADENCE

The teacher explained the next quiz would be on ethical violations and SEC rules. I closed the book, and he dismissed the class for the day. Finally, I could relax and grab a cup of coffee before I went home to study until dinner. Gunner's planned a nice dinner with our friends, and I wanted to be rested after the night we stayed up with Kyrin. That boy of mine loved his Marvel movies, and I could remember every line that Thor said with the amount of times we watched his movies. I hopped in my car and headed to the coffee shop next to the school. It was fairly quiet, and as I moved up in line to place my order, I felt a tap on my shoulder.

"Rosaline."

"I thought that was you, Kadence." Rosaline extended her arm for a hug.

"What are you doing here?"

"I saw you come in when I passed by. How are things at Club Seek?" Rosaline tossed her blond hair to the side, and I whirled around to give my order.

"Can I get the vanilla latte please? Things are good. I haven't seen you around."

Rosaline's eyes racked over me.

"They weren't paying me enough, so I left."

I found that hard to believe, because Mason and Gunner said the place had the wealthiest clientele, but I didn't question her further.

"Sorry to hear that."

"No worries. I'm making a ton of money at my new place. But how is everyone?" She walked alongside me to wait for my order.

"Everybody is good." The barista passed me my drink order, and I grabbed a straw.

"Is Gunner seeing anyone?" she asked, and my face scrunched up in confusion.

"Gunner?"

"Yeah, we were talking a little, but after I left, he got mad and cut me off," Rosaline lied, and I wanted to mention our relationship. I didn't like confrontation in public.

"Huh, I have to go, Rosaline. It was good to see you." I rushed out of the cafe and ran to my car.

Ring!

I saw Emma's number flash across the screen.

"Hello." I drove out of the cafe.

"What is Gunner planning for dinner? I need to know what I should wear."

"Uhm, Emma, I can't really talk right now."

"Why? What's wrong?"

"I think Gunner is cheating or was seeing someone."

"Huh, slow down. Where are you?"

"Driving. I just left school and ran into Rosaline."

"Who's Rosaline?"

"I used to work with her at the club." I came to a stop sign and placed my drink in the holder.

"Okay, and how does she factor into your relationship?"

"She asked if Gunner is dating anybody."

"What did you say?"

"I was surprised when she said they dated, and I rushed out of there."

Emma got quiet.

"Look, Kadence, some women are jealous. She probably knows you're seeing him and set that meeting up."

"Rosaline wouldn't do that."

"How close are you to her?"

"Not really close, but we've talked at work a few times."

"Then you have no loyalties to her, only Gunner. I say ignore her."

"Emma, you say that about anything." I chortled and drove toward my apartment.

"Anyway, do you think casual jeans and blouses would work?"

I picked up my things, climbed out of the car, and locked the door.

"Yeah, that should work. Nothing major. We'll have drinks and dinner on the patio." I unlocked my apartment door, reached for my mail on the ground, and picked it up.

"Sounds good. See you in a little while, babe.

"You too, crazy lady."

I dropped the mail on the table and blew out a breath. I sat on the couch, rubbing my temples.

"Gunner and Rosaline dated," I muttered to myself.

* * *

CONVERSATION FLOWED and drinks poured as Emma continued to talk about the way her son acted in daycare today. Jordan came out, and I was glad to see them reconnect again and make their marriage a priority. In the past, my marriage had a bumpy road, but we came out on the right side of things until his death. My head whirled around to Gunner when he rubbed my neck and kissed me on the shoulder.

"You seem quiet tonight."

"I'm fine." I lifted my glass and drank the champagne.

"Come with me." Gunner stood and grabbed my hand. I looked at him in confusion.

"Where?"

"We'll be right back, everyone," Gunner explained, and Emma peered at me. I waved her off and put my napkin down. Gunner walked me to his massive kitchen, and I removed my hand and stared off. His eyes were on me.

"Are you upset with me?" He pulled my hands apart and laid them on his chest.

"Rosaline asked about you."

His mouth turned downward.

"Where did you see Rosaline?"

"Are you still sleeping with her?" My body went tense with shock.

"Kadence."

"You know what? Don't answer, I need to go." I felt a clutch of panic in the pit of my stomach.

I angled around him and stormed out of the kitchen, passing our friends to get my jacket and purse. Emma and Chelsey jumped up to follow us.

"You told him," Emma commented, and he looked between us.

"I'll call you later, Emma. Nice seeing you again, Chelsey."

"Kadence! Kadence!" Gunner yelled after me. I raised my hand up to protest him from following, hopped in my car, and left.

Ring! Ring!

I switched my phone to Do Not Disturb to stop his incessant calls and sped into traffic. If he couldn't answer a simple question, there was something to them dating. When I finally pulled up to my apartment and parked, my door was yanked open.

"Oh my God!" I jerked back, and Gunner stood at my door. "Get out of the car. Gunner, go home." I grabbed my purse and stepped around him. All of a sudden, I was lifted off the ground and thrown over his shoulder. "Gunner! Put me down." I smacked him on the back.

"Shut up." He smacked my ass, took my keys out of my hand, and unlocked my apartment door.

We walked inside, and he put me on his lap. I avoided eye contact until he gripped my chin to face him.

"Listen to me," he shot back, his eyes glittering with anger.

"I told you I needed a minute."

"No, you just left without hearing me out."

"It doesn't matter."

"It does to me, and you're listening to someone I haven't spoken to in months."

"She's…"

"She's irrelevant, Kadence. A girl I hooked up with a few times in the past."

He laid a hand on my thigh and squeezed.

"Based on how she questioned me earlier, I doubt you're irrelevant to her." I nudged his hand off my leg.

Gunner smiled and sat back on the couch.

"Are you scared?"

"What?"

"Of what we could be?"

"Gunner—" He stopped me.

"No, you and I click, and you're trying to force the

Rosaline thing to end us before we really get started. I know you lost your husband, and your in-laws aren't reliable. But I'm not them."

His words were true, and I did keep people at arm's length after everything I'd gone through in life. Plus, my parents weren't the best example of commitment.

"All right, so Rosaline is in her head about you two being more than you are?"

"She and I had no real ties, baby. It's been you from the moment I saw you."

I smirked and leaned up against his chest. We kissed, and I jerked back in thought.

"Your dinner."

He chuckled.

"Come on, let's head back to my place."

"I know they probably think I'm crazy."

"Emma wanted to come with the girls and drag you back, but I said to let me handle it instead."

I covered my face in embarrassment.

"I'm sorry."

He kissed my forehead.

"No apologies necessary. I like this jealousy on you."

I smacked him gently on the chest.

"Whatever, Mr. Vishon," I joked, and he smacked me on the ass.

CHAPTER EIGHT

GUNNER

Knock! Knock!

"It's open!" I shuffled some papers on my desk and piled them for my assistant to file when Rosaline stepped into my office. Two days ago, Kadence came to me upset and ready to break things off. I was pissed off at the time, but I didn't want to show my hand and have her think I was a crazy asshole. Rosaline pushed me too far in contacting Kadence, like we had a relationship.

"I knew you'd call again."

Rosaline started to walk around my desk.

"Have a seat." I motioned to the chair in front of my desk.

"You seem upset, baby." Rosaline crossed her legs and bit her bottom lip flirtatiously.

"Rosaline, what's the problem?"

"Huh?"

"You told Kadence we were in a relationship?"

"Kadence, Kadence at the club?"

"Yeah."

"Why do you care what I told her?"

"She's my girl."

"Since when?" She jumped up with a frown on her face.

"None of your business, but you and I have never made any commitment to be together."

"Not in words, but the way you—" I stopped her before she could lie.

"Have I taken you to dinner?"

"No."

"Have I introduced you to a friend?"

"No, but Gunner…"

"Rosaline, I'm only saying this once. We are done."

Her nostrils flared, and her fists balled up.

"Fuck you, Gunner!" She snatched up her purse and stormed out of my office.

I fell back in my chair and ran a hand down my face. Rosaline knew what was best for her. She'd move on. I picked up my cell and made plans to show Kadence I was serious about us.

"Hey, baby."

"How are you?" Kadence asked.

"Wonderful. How are you doing? You didn't sleep in my bed last night. I missed you."

She giggled through the line.

"Kyrin had a fever."

"Do you need me to bring anything?"

"No. He's almost over it now. How is work?"

"Work is work, same shit different day." I kicked my feet up on the desk.

"Sounds like you're busy."

"I was, but not anymore."

"Maybe you want to come over for lunch."

"I'd like that, but how about I take you and Kyrin out for lunch? My treat."

"You don't have to do that, Gunner."

"I want to. Besides, I haven't seen my bestie."

"Here you go."

I laughed. Kyrin and I had a secret handshake and became best friends. Kadence hated when we would watch cartoons and play with his train set scattered over her living room.

"Is my baby jealous?"

"Shut up, Gunner, and I'll see you soon."

"What do you think about the club tonight?" With both our schedules, we hadn't had time to indulge, but I wanted to make up for the situation with Rosaline and devote all my time to Kadence to show her I was serious about us.

"I'd love to go," she cooed, and my dick stiffened in my pants.

"See you in a few."

* * *

KYRIN WAS MUCH BETTER after being sick, so after lunch, we took him to the park. He climbed up the play ladder and slid back down to follow some more kids.

"He's better." I pointed at Kyrin jumping on the swing.

"Finally. These last few days were crazy."

I covered her palm.

"I talked with Rosaline."

"And what did she say?"

"She couldn't say anything. I told her to keep my name out of her mouth."

"I guess you're stuck with me then." Kadence laid her head on my shoulder.

"The best person to be stuck with."

"Gunner! Come push me on the swings," Kyrin yelled from the swings.

"What about me?" Kadence joked as she stood.

"Mommy, you're always here. I want Gunner to push me."

I laughed at their back-and-forth, raised my arm around her neck, and kissed her forehead.

"Sorry, love. He wants the best." Kadence pushed me off, and I laughed, jogging to Kyrin to push him on the swing.

"Smile. I want a picture," Kadence called out, and I held Kyrin in the swing. The rest of the day was spent with Kyrin in the park. Then we went to grab ice cream and his favorite pizza for dinner.

CHAPTER NINE

KADENCE

Gunner secured the private emerald room tonight. My arms circled his neck, and I deepened the kiss; then he leaned back.

"What's wrong?"

"I'm running the show." He removed my dress and helped me take off his clothes.

Gunner hungrily kissed me, then released me and captured my hand to walk me to the bed we often used when I had a night off. I went to sit, and he shook his head and turned me to face him.

"Tonight's a little different."

"How so?"

"I want you lying on the spreader over in the corner."

I smirked and reached out to grasp his dick.

"Is this pleasure or punishment tonight?"

"Both."

Gunner helped me to climb on top. I raised my arms above my head, and locked them in place. He did the same to my legs and had them at an angle that he could stand in the middle with his face directly in front of my pussy.

"Gunner…" I felt my stomach stir in anticipation.

"Shussh."

He picked up the vibrator, held it up to my face and then lifted the flogger. I licked my lips, ready for his games.

"I want all of you tonight."

"Yes."

He gripped his dick and stroked himself.

"Fuck! You're lying down like that, sexy and willing."

"I want you in my mouth."

"It's coming." Gunner turned the vibrator on to a medium setting and pushed around my nipple, then my breast. He used his other hand to jerk off in front of me. I hated not being able to touch him.

"Gunner, please." He moved the vibrator to my mouth and pushed it in and out. Our eyes connected and I felt my wetness.

"Mmmmm," I moaned. He maneuvered the vibrator to my pussy and replaced it with his dick.

"Oh fuck, baby. Take it slow."

He caressed my cheek and watched the vibrator enter my lower lips. Gunner turned the vibrator up a little, and I felt an overwhelming sensation. Warmth swarmed through my body.

"So wet."

I was so ready to pass out from all of the sensations. Gunner removed his thick shaft and kissed me on the lips.

"I want to touch you."

"Not yet."

He removed the vibrator, slid into me, and buried his face in my neck. Sucking on my ear, I felt his warm breath along my neck and shoulder. We made eye contact, and I saw the satisfaction in his eyes. His hand went to rub my clit, and my eyes rolled to the back of my head.

My back slightly arched, and we fucked for the next two hours.

* * *

WE WERE COMING up on six months of dating, and I hadn't been this happy in a long time. After dropping Kyrin at daycare, I told the girls I wanted to catch up. All of us had busy lives, and I wanted to show them the progress I'd made with school plans and Kyrin. I waved at Kyra when I approached the table and reached down to hug her and Emma.

"You're all done up. Did you have a shoot today?"

"Yes, and Warren is taking me out to dinner tonight, so I have to stay ready," Kyra teased.

I sat in the booth, opposite to Kyra and Emma.

"What is this glow on you?" Emma questioned.

"Life is good."

"Life or dick?" Emma joked.

"Girl!" We high-fived.

"Both, and my baby is doing well. Plus, my classes are going well."

"So happy to hear that. Has Kyrin been okay with having a man around the house?"

"He has. I made sure to take it slow and not just spring a new person on him."

"What about your mom?"

"Haven't talked to her in a few weeks."

"Why not?"

"She's been standoffish. Plus, Gunner and I have Kyrin most of the time."

"Oohh."

"Never would replace his father, but Gunner has shown himself to be a great friend."

"I like him for you," Emma said.

"I like him too." I smiled.

"Are you planning on staying at the club?" Kyra questioned.

"Not forever, but once school is done, I can look for a job in the administration field or start my own business."

"I'm surprised Gunner hasn't said anything about you quitting," Kyra said as she sipped her strawberry soda.

"He never brought it up like it was a bad thing." I shrugged.

"He can't say anything. He found his fling there," Emma commented.

"True, but how are you and Jordan doing? Enough talk about me."

"Happily married and ready for more kids." Emma raised her hand and showed off the new wedding ring.

"Jordan showed out on this ring."

"Yes, my husband is fabulous, isn't he?" Emma joked.

"What about you, Kyra?"

"Working and dealing with Warren's crazy self."

"What did he do now?"

"Driving me crazy about having a baby." Kyra sighed.

"He just loves you and wants to have a mini diva running around." I laughed.

CHAPTER TEN

KADENCE

The next day.

Kyrin ran inside my mom's house, and I laughed at him. Bypassing her toward the TV, he pulled out his toys. The talk with the girls helped me to get the courage to visit my mom and try to get on the same page, for Kyrin's sake at least.

"Hi."

"Hey, is he staying?" She shut the door behind me.

"If you want him to."

"He's my grandbaby, why wouldn't I?"

"Can we talk without the sass, Mom?"

"Kadence, shut up."

She pulled out a cigarette and lit it up.

"Why are you so angry with me?"

"I'm not angry with you."

"Then what is with the attitude all the time?"

She glanced at Kyrin, then back at me.

"You look just like your father."

"Here we go."

"See that's your problem now, always rolling eyes."

"Ma, I'm not Daddy."

"You think I don't know that."

She headed to the kitchen, and I followed. I climbed up on the counter and watched as she washed the dishes.

"He was an asshole."

"To you."

"You too. You just don't remember."

"You have to get over him."

"Who's the mother in this relationship?"

"Okay." I picked the towel up to dry the dishes.

"I just didn't have the life I wanted, and I do have some regrets, I took out my anger on you," she mumbled.

"I figured."

"You're doing great for yourself, and I guess I envied you."

"You can always go back to school."

"I'm too old."

"You're never too old to follow your dreams, Mom."

"How is that boyfriend of yours?"

"He's fine."

"He's cute."

"Thanks. When did you see him?"

"When you dropped Kyrin off months back, he was in the car."

"Oh."

"I'm glad you've opened your heart, Kadence."

"Thanks. I wish I could say the same for you."

She waved me off.

"Men are only good for one thing."

"What's that?"

"Money." She burst into laughter.

"Not even sex?"

"Honey, I got a toy upstairs that does me fine."

"All right, I don't need to know that." I pretended to throw up.

"Are you working tonight?"

"Yeah and some studying."

"Well, get on out of here and get to work. Tell that boyfriend of yours don't be a stranger."

I jumped off the counter and kissed her cheek. We hugged; and then she walked me to the living room. I bent down to kiss Kyrin on the top of his head and told him I was leaving. I strolled out of her apartment and grabbed my phone to call Gunner.

CHAPTER ELEVEN

KADENCE

"Oh, fuck!" I cried out, trying to grab the back of Gunner's head. As my hands were tied, he snaked his tongue in my lower lips. I squeezed my eyes shut as the feel of his large hands ran across my stomach. Gunner flicked my nipple, pinched, and moved to my right breast. The ice chips sat in the bucket, and I knew the torture was about to begin.

"What are the rules, Kadence?"

"Pick up when you call." I looked down at his hand gripping my thigh.

"What else?" He smacked, then squeezed my left breast.

"Stop allowing people that don't matter in my life to upset me."

"What did you do today?"

He stopped sucking on my pearl, and I was pissed.

"I reached out to Kyrin's grandparents."

"They ignored your calls once again, baby."

"I know."

"So, what should your punishment be?"

He crawled up my body and hovered over me.

"Two orgasms minimum," I joked, and he chuckled, reaching for a piece of ice from the bucket.

"I should say no orgasms, but that would deprive me as well."

"They don't deserve me."

"Exactly. You're special, and anyone who doesn't see that can fuck off." He pressed the ice against my bottom lips and rubbed against my top. I stuck my tongue out and licked his finger as he held it in my mouth.

"Gunner." I gasped when he pressed the ice on my nipple and rubbed around my areola.

"She's pointed right at me, waiting to be sucked." Gunner stared at my breasts.

"Fuck me."

"We're together. You're everything to me, and no one will change that."

"I know, baby!" I cooed. He ran the ice down my stomach, circled my navel and then against my lower lips.

"Shit, she's ready for me." He pushed the ice in, lowered his head, and sucked on the ice. It felt so good as it melted with his mouth combating the coolness of the ice.

"Wet and ready, baby."

"Ouu… Shit! Yes, Gunner," I hollered, twisting my head back and forth. My chest rapidly rose and my breathing heightened.

"Your pussy's calling my name, Kadence." He slid a finger in and out.

"Gunner! Please put it in and make love to me."

He smirked, stood, and removed his pants and shirt. He grabbed the blindfold from the nightstand and placed it over my eyes.

"What are you doing?"

"Making our night special. I want you to just remember

through my touch." He lifted my legs and spread them out more. I felt the head of his pole tap against my slit.

"Shit, you're already soaking the sheets." Gunner didn't just slide in, but grinded slowly back and forth. My swollen clit screamed for him, and he teased me for minutes, but it felt like hours.

"I need you inside me."

"I like when you beg." His husky voice whispered in my ear. When he thrusted forward, he buried his dick deep between my walls. We stayed like that for a few seconds, and his groans against my ear only caused me to get wetter.

"Never again will I allow anyone to hurt you." He sounded pissed and ready to fight all my battles as he pounded with long strokes. My mouth stretched open at a loss for words.

"Yes! Baby, Fuck!" I cried out when he pushed my legs up to my chest.

"Fuck! You. Are. Everything. To. Me. Kadence." Gunner slowed his strokes, lay on my chest, removed the mask, and pulled my lips to his. We made love for the rest of the night at the club.

CHAPTER TWELVE

GUNNER

"*D*id you tell them about Kyrin?"

I parked the car and turned to face her.

"Babe, you need to relax."

"Gunner."

I lifted her hand and kissed the back of her palm.

"I know your other in-laws aren't supportive."

She scoffed at my words.

"Try evil." She leaned her head against the headrest.

"My parents aren't like that. I promise, and if they were, I wouldn't bring you around."

"They fooled me in the beginning."

"Billy and Katy Vishon aren't good actors." I lifted her chin and pressed a kiss on her lips.

Kadence turned her head and smiled.

"Well, they better be nice because I'd hate to lose this." She reached over and gripped my dick.

"Maybe we can reschedule this dinner and go back to my place."

She laughed, and I sucked her bottom lip.

"Nope, dinner first."

I opened the door and jogged around to help her out. We strolled to the front door, and my mother opened it and outstretched her arms.

"I was wondering when you'd show up."

After giving my mom a hug, I moved to the side and introduced Kadence.

"This is Kadence, my girlfriend."

"Nice to meet you, Kadence. I'm Katy," Mom said and leaned in for a hug.

"You too, Mrs. Vishon."

She waved her comment off.

"Please call me Katy."

"Katy."

"Come in. Are you thirsty? I have wine, water, beer, or soda." Our family was the typical family that let all the kids hang out at their house. Most parents had rules and never let their children experience anything, but Mom and Dad kept the communication open and explained about what drugs and alcohol could do if we abused them. I followed in my dad's footsteps when it came to business and became an entrepreneur. Mom worked as a paralegal, and Dad owned an investment firm and his own sporting goods store.

"Water is fine."

"Gunner, are you having beer?" Mom asked.

"Please. Where's Dad?" I removed my jacket and laid it on the seat of the couch.

"Should be coming in from the store any minute."

"How is the store doing?" I took the beer out of her hands, and Kadence thanked her for the glass of water.

"The store is busy. He might open another one." She sat on the opposite side of us.

The door opened, and Dad walked in with a newspaper in his hand.

"Gunner! Who is this lovely lady?" Dad dropped the newspaper on the table and leaned over to kiss my mom on the lips.

"Kadence, my girlfriend. You look like a tired old man." I stood and shook his hand.

He went into a boxing stance, and I laughed.

"Your old man can still last a few rounds." He chuckled.

"Hi, Mr. Vishon. I'm Kadence."

"Please call me Billy. Sit back down."

"I was just telling Kadence to call me Katy."

"My son tells me you're in school." Dad grabbed the beer from my mom's hand and took a sip.

"I have about two years left. Then I get my degree in business."

"Nice. I like a smart woman. You did good, Gunner." He winked.

"Tell us about yourself, Kadence. Gunner mentioned you have a son."

"Yes, a little boy. After my husband died, I'm raising him on my own."

"Sorry to hear that. You'll have to bring him around. We have a huge pool in the back," Mom explained.

"I think Kyrin will probably never leave your house," Kadence kidded.

"We've been wanting grandkids for the longest time, so this will give us practice." Dad took another sip.

"So, you're a widower?"

Kadence encircled my hand.

"It's only been a year and a half, so it's tough for me to bring up."

"Understandable. I can relate," my mom said.

"How?" I questioned.

"We never talked about this, Gunner, but I was married before your father." My eyes ballooned.

"What? I never knew this."

"I was young and met your father a few years after. But he was a good man who died from a car accident," Mom explained.

"Yeah, I met your mom years down the road. We became friends and eventually, I fell in love with her," Dad said.

"Learn something new every day."

"Come on, let's go eat. Then we can show you pictures of Gunner when he was younger." We all stood and walked into the dining room. I stopped Kadence and wrapped my arms around her waist in the hallway.

"Any regret?"

"None. What about you?"

"None."

"Then let's go eat with your parents and plan our future family nights together. I bet Kyrin is going to like your parents more than me." Kadence cupped both sides of my face and kissed me.

EPILOGUE

GUNNER

A year and a half later.

Kadence held up her diploma and took pictures with her friends, then with her son and mom. It was great to stand back and watch her finally get everything she deserved and not have to struggle or fight for support. The promise I made and committed was to be there for her throughout, and so far, it'd been that way. Kyrin didn't seem fazed about moving in with me and starting a new life as long as he had his own room and pizza night. I laughed at the thought of him trying to negotiate pizza night every day before he agreed with the move. I respected how Kadence handled everything with her in-laws when they tried to come back into his life and demanded they work on earning her trust before she put Kyrin in a situation to be disappointed. My parents came up next and stood for a picture with her, and I chuckled at how much I loved that Kyrin embraced my family. Already he enjoyed spending time with my dad because he let him have all the candy he wanted when he visited.

"Babe, you ready?" Kadence approached me.

"Yeah, do we have to swing by the house for anything?"

"No, the restaurant has everything organized." Kadence slipped her hand in mine. Kyrin ran to us, and I bent down to pick him up.

"Do you want pizza Kyrin?" I asked.

"Yes! And—"

"No pizza, Kyrin! We're having a real meal as a family," Kadence replied, reaching for him.

Kyrin threw his hands up in the air, and we both laughed.

"He's so spoiled." Kadence rubbed his head.

Kyrin would try to run anything if you let him. It was funny to see how Kadence interacted with him. Something I could see for our future children. We walked to my car and gathered everyone to announce the plans for the rest of the day.

"Follow us to the restaurant," I said to my parents after I helped Kyrin in the car seat.

"Babe, I have a surprise for you." Kadence grabbed my hand across the seat.

"Today is about you and your graduation."

"I know, but I couldn't wait."

"What's the surprise?"

"We can save it for later, but just be prepared for the club."

My heart fluttered at her request. The last time we went, she allowed me to explore her for hours, and I was waiting for her to officially quit working at the club and feel more comfortable with being a member.

"So, you're ready to become a member?"

"I'm ready for anything."

We ended up at the restaurant, and Kadence had reserved a private section. It was nice to see her with a smile on her face and a glow on her skin from accomplishing her goal. Emma stood up with her champagne.

"I want to make a toast," Emma said.

"Don't make me cry, Emma." Kadence poked out her lip.

I raised my arm on the back of her chair.

"Too late," Maya joked.

"Hush, Maya." Emma cleared her throat.

"We love your speeches, babe," Jordan responded, rubbing her back.

Emma grinned.

"To Kadence, you've shined and overcome obstacles while raising a beautiful young boy. You're an inspiration to us all." Emma held her glass up, and everybody clinked glasses.

I pulled Kadence into my arms and kissed her on the cheek.

"You've earned this, babe," I whispered in her ear.

"I know, and I appreciate you for being patient with me."

"Trust me, you're worth being patient for, baby."

Kyrin ran over to us, and I pulled him on my lap, and we played with his trucks. Kadence talked with her friends, and the evening was like a reunion of family and friends. Once the dinner was finished, Kyrin went to Emma's for the night, and I planned to take Kadence on a getaway with just the two of us as a present for all her hard work. She wasn't only a mother, friend, daughter, and girlfriend, but hopefully, she'd become a wife again. In life, we lived for the moments and experiences. When death hits, it shocks us into not wanting to love again. For Kadence, I wanted to show her that it was about the memories one made that mattered and carried on. Even though she lost a love, I would never replace him or take away that experience. I only wanted to add more memories of joy.

* * *

I HOPE you enjoyed Kadence and Gunner's story. Also check out where it all begins with "**Wet Heat**," a best friend's brother's romance.

Don't forget if you love Fling romances, bodyguard, forced proximity then check out, "**Protecting Chanel**" https://books2read.com/u/mqwPB8

If you love brother's best friend romance, then you'll love "**Sensual**" **here** https://books2read.com/u/49lYYM with a dash of steamy romance.

Check out Bodyguard Romance, military, romantic suspense here *"Protecting Bria"* https://books2read.com/u/bQJkjd

How about a steamy, medical romance? Check out *"Haven"* https://books2read.com/u/4jAvyZ a steamy enemies to lovers romance.

Have you checked out "**His Peace Her Pleasure**"? Click here https://books2read.com/u/3JJr0P a billionaire, steamy romance.

Please also check out my *"Love Don't Live here Anymore"* https://books2read.com/u/mBOWGZ a steamy enemies to lovers romance.

ABOUT THE AUTHOR

A TENNESSEE NATIVE, AND California dreaming Author KeKe Renée is living and striving to continue her passion of writing short story romances in genres ranging from Erotic, Paranormal, and Women's Fiction.

304 PUBLISHING COMPANY

WE SHOWCASE AUTHORS WRITING African American, Interracial, Women's Fiction, Urban Romance, Erotic, and Contemporary Romance novels. Along with Thriller, Suspense, Poetry, Beauty, and Style Books. Thank you for taking the time out to visit. Join our mailing list to stay updated with new releases and blog posts.

WANT TO KNOW WHAT happens next?

Follow me on Bookbub and social media today.

Reviews are the lifeblood of the publishing world. They're read, appreciated, and needed. Please consider taking the time to leave a few words on wherever you buy books. Sign up for updates and sneak peeks at the site below.

CATALOG OF RELEASES BY KEKE RENÉE:

- Wet Heat (Wet Heat Series Book 1)
- Every Time We Touch Novelette (Wet Heat Book 2 Series)
- His Peace, Her Pleasure
- Baby, It's Cold Outside
- Love Don't Live Here Anymore, Vanessa Andrew Book 1
- Love Don't Live Here Anymore, Isabella Andrew Book2
- One Night Only-A Novelette (Love By Design Book 1)
- Cassian and Savannah (Love By Design Book 2)
- Deidra's Love (Love By Design Book 3)
- Protecting Bria (Special Force Operation Alphas)
- Sensual
- Seek To Please Book 1
- Seek To Touch Book 2
- Seek To Bare Book 3
- Seek To Love Book 4
- Protecting Chanel (Special Forces Operation Alphas)

- Seek To Trust Book 5
- Seek To Earn Book 6

Thank you so much for reading, and if you enjoyed the crazy ride and decide to leave a review we'd truly appreciate the support.

www.ingramcontent.com/pod-product-compliance
Lightning Source LLC
Chambersburg PA
CBHW051802130726
47987CB00003B/1074